This book belongs to: ______________________________

The Wandering Walnut
Title of the original edition: Die wandernde Nuss
Copyright Text © Marina Kramer, 2021
Copyright Illustration © Marina Kramer, 2021
mh-books@gmx.de
Marina Krämer, 71732 Tamm
Translated from the German by Tanya Laurenson
Independently published

The present work, including individual parts, is protected by copyright.
All rights reserved by the author.

# The Wandering Walnut

**Marina Kramer**

Translated by Tanya Laurenson

Once upon a time there was a walnut.
It fell from the tree – right in front of a squirrel.

"You'll be a great treat this winter," said the squirrel as it buried the walnut in the ground.

“What‘s that wonderful smell?”

The mole sniffed the walnut and took it into his pantry.

"At last, something tasty to munch on," said the wild boar with delight as it scrabbled about after the walnut.

The walnut then rolled into the undergrowth...

**...right under the nose of a dozing weasel.**

"I've always dreamed of having a ball as good as this one!" said the Weasel with excitement, as it kicked the walnut...

...into the river.

"You're scaring away all my fishes, you good-for-nothing!" whistled the kingfisher, outraged. And, with one blow, he batted the walnut onto the river bank.

**“I don‘t need you here, you silly stone!” complained the badger, and threw the walnut away.**

The nut flew...

...and hit a mouse directly on the head.

**“Ouch! You silly nut!” complained the mouse and stamped the walnut into the moss in anger.**

**The walnut stayed there for a very long time...**

One day, the squirrel came along and was amazed to see a magnificent walnut tree.

**All of a sudden, a walnut fell from the tree – right in front of...**

**Help the walnut find its way to the animals.**

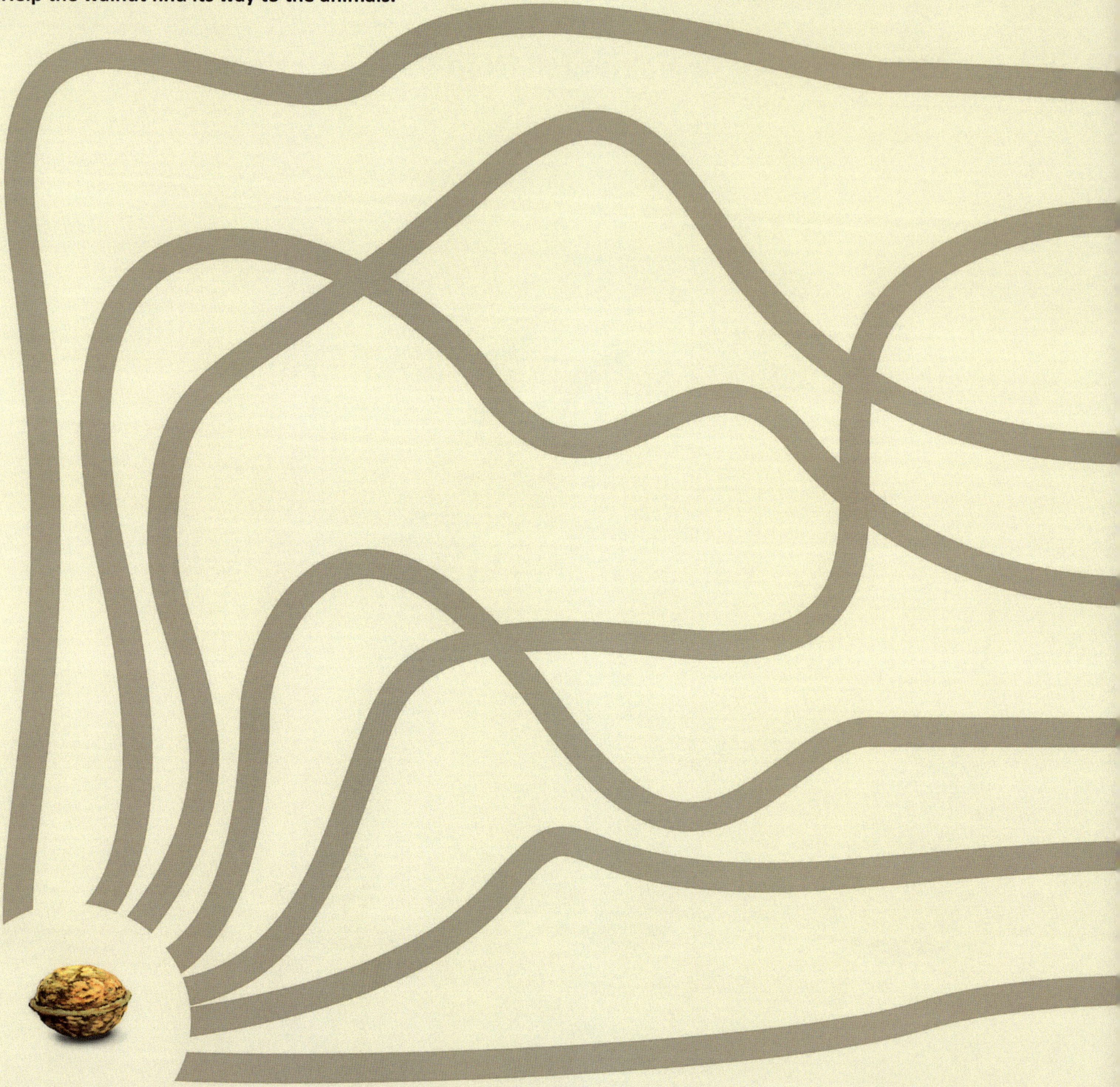

Printed in Poland
by Amazon Fulfillment
Poland Sp. z o.o., Wrocław

35197055R00016